CONTENTS

Introduction

A new Age of Dragons is about to begin. The **powerful** creatures will return to rule the **world** once more, but this time it will be **different**. This time, they will have allies who will **help** them. Around the world, some young humans are making a strange **discovery**. They are learning that they were born with **dragon blood** – blood that gives them **amazing powers**.

CHAPTER 1

Dragon on Paper

A young man named Henry sat on a bus, drawing a picture.

"Hey, what's that?" asked another passenger.

"Um, it's nothing," said the young man.

The passenger grabbed the pad of paper away from Henry.

HA! HA!

He stared at the picture and *laughed*.

"Is this what you think is happening to all those stolen cars?" asked the man.

Henry shrugged.

The man returned the pad to Henry.

"Well, who knows?" said the man. "Your guess is as good as anyone else's."

CHAPTER 2
Missing Cars

Henry got off the bus at the next stop.

The buildings were dark.

The *streetlights* flickered on and off.

Henry had not been in this part of the city before.

A *breeze* blew a dirty newspaper against his legs.

He reached down and grabbed the paper.

The headlines were about the car thieves again.

All over the city, cars were

disappearing.

No one knew how it was done,
or who the thieves were.

Henry had been having dreams
about the disappearing cars.

In his dreams, a strange flying creature grabbed them.

But Henry had come to the city searching for something else.

Something that was missing.

He was not looking for the lost cars.

Henry was looking for his friend.

CHAPTER 3
Blood Brothers

16

Last summer, Henry and his friend Matt became blood brothers.

Henry had seen it done on a TV programme.

He and Matt both pricked their thumbs with a needle.

Bright blood appeared.

Then they touched thumbs and shook hands.

"We're **blood** brothers now," said Matt.

"Brothers forever," said Henry.

Matt's mother walked by the door to his room.

She saw the blood and screamed.

"What do you boys think you're doing?" she yelled.

"Blood can be dangerous!" she cried.

"People get sick from other people's blood," she added.

"We're blood brothers now," explained Matt.

Henry had to leave. Matt was in big trouble with his mum.

For the rest of the summer, the two boys didn't see each other.

CHAPTER 4
Rooftops

Now, Henry stared down at his pad of paper.

Henry had a strange feeling.

He was sure that Matt was somewhere in the city.

He was also sure that his dream held a clue to finding his friend.

Henry stared at the picture again. Then he *looked* up.

High above him, the building's roof had a strange antenna.

It was the same antenna as the one in his picture.

It was the same antenna he had seen in his dreams.

Henry found a door that led into
the building.

He climbed a set of steep stairs.

Minutes later, Henry opened a
rusty, metal door.

He was standing on the roof of
the building.

CHAPTER 5
The Nest

A huge pile of smashed cars lay on the roof.

These are the missing cars, thought Henry.

Just then, a **huge** shape rose up from the cars.

It shook its **wings** and yawned.

Henry stared at the **dragon.**

Its *yellow eyes* blinked at Henry.

The creature opened its jaws and
screamed.

Henry dropped his pad of paper.

His body **trembled**.

Wings began to sprout from his

shoulders.

Soon there were two **dragons** on the rooftop.

They stood facing each other.

They each lifted a claw and then pressed them together.

The two dragons flapped their wings and flew into the grey sky.

Brothers forever.

Of Dragons and Near-Dragons

Lizards are a common sight in cities, as well as in deserts and jungles. Asian house geckos are common in houses and hotels. They walk on walls and ceilings. Green iguanas can be found on rooftops and on the side of roads.

Mediterranean geckos are widespread in parts of Texas. They can be found around homes and other buildings. This same species lives in Oklahoma, Arizona, Mexico, and the Caribbean.

The black spitting cobra can be found in the urban areas of Singapore. The snake hunts at night, eating pesky mice and rats. Sometimes, the cobra even slithers inside peoples' houses!

Australian cities have the biggest residential lizards in the world. Lizards around 60 centimetres (23 inches) long are a common sight in gardens and backyards. Luckily, there are no poisonous lizards in Australia.

The northern curly-tailed lizard has made its home in southern Florida. This creature can be found at shopping centres, carparks, and many other places around town. It is called the "T. rex of ground lizards," and likes to snuggle up against warm cement.

ABOUT THE AUTHOR

Michael Dahl is the author of more than 200 books for children and young adults. He has won the AEP Distinguished Achievement Award three times for his non-fiction. His *Finnegan Zwake* mystery series was shortlisted twice by the Anthony and Agatha awards. He has also written the *Library of Doom* series. He is a featured speaker at conferences around the country on graphic novels and high-interest books for boys.

ABOUT THE ILLUSTRATOR

Yap Kun Rong is a freelance illustrator and concept artist for books, comics, and video games.

GLOSSARY

allies people or countries that give support to each other

creature living thing that is human or animal

dangerous likely to cause harm or injury

flickered blinked or moved unsteadily

passenger someone besides the driver who travels in a car or other vehicle

pricked made a small hole

rule have power over something

sprout grow, appear, or develop quickly

steep rising very sharply

DISCUSSION QUESTIONS

1. Was it right for the man on the bus to grab Henry's drawing? Have you ever been in a similar situation?

2. Why did Matt's mum get so angry when Matt and Henry became blood brothers?

3. Was Matt or Henry the original dragon? Explain your answer.

WRITING PROMPTS

1. Henry had a very detailed dream. Write about your favourite dream.

2. What did you think was happening to all of the cars that were disappearing? Write three different explanations for the missing cars.

3. At the end of the story, Matt and Henry fly off together. Is that really the end? Write another chapter to the book describing where Matt and Henry go.

MORE BOOKS TO READ

LIBRARY OF DOOM

Meet the mysterious Librarian. Keeper of the world's most dangerous books, sworn enemy of monsters made of paper and ink, crusader of young people threatened by ancient curses... Enter the Library of Doom to follow these heart-pounding adventures.